Disney's

DISNEY'S

Adapted from the film by A. L. Singer

New York

1 3 5 7 9 10 8 6 4 2

Library of Congress Catalog Card Number: 91-73806

ISBN: 1-56282-138-5

Disney's Robin Hood

CHAPTER ONE

sk anyone about Robin Hood, and this is what you'll hear:

He robbed from the rich and gave to the poor.

He lived with a band of Merry Men in Sherwood Forest.

He outfoxed the wicked Sheriff of Nottingham.

Well, all those things are true. But there's more to Robin Hood than that. Much more. Take it from me, we folks in the animal kingdom know the *real* story.

Who am I? Why, my name is Allan-a-Dale, and I'm a minstrel. I'm also an old friend of Robin's. That's right. Sure, I'm a rooster and Robin's a fox, but that never stopped us from being pals.

Let me tell you about Robin's greatest adventure. It all began long, long ago in England. King Richard was on the throne back then, and he was a kind man. He ruled fairly, and everybody liked him. But one day he left England to go on a long journey to the Holy Land, and his brother John became ruler.

That was when all the trouble started.

Prince John was, well, *rotten*. He loved only two things—himself and money. He made his subjects pay him so much tax that they became poor.

People tried to hold on to their money, but they couldn't. Not when the Sheriff of Nottingham was around! The sheriff was a fat old wolf who went from house to house collecting taxes for Prince John. Some people called him Bushel Britches—but never to his face, of course. If you had any money lying around—even a penny—the sheriff would just take it.

And he was determined to catch Robin Hood.

These were hard times. Many families would have starved if it wasn't for Robin Hood. Somehow he would always manage to sneak by the sheriff's men and bring the poor folk the money he had stolen from the rich.

Take the time Prince John was traveling through Sherwood Forest. Now, the prince was a lion who knew how to travel in style. His coach was pulled along by four huge rhinos. Inside, he sat on a throne surrounded by plush curtains. Six elephants led the way, trumpeting the prince's presence. *Rat-ta-ta-ta-ta-taahhh!*

It just so happened that Robin Hood was in the forest that day with his trusted companion, Little John. Little John was the friendliest bear you'd ever want to meet, though you might say he was a bit . . . clumsy.

Well, clumsy or not, Little John followed Robin up a tree like a squirrel when they heard the prince coming.

"Ho-ho!" Robin whispered as the trumpeting elephants came nearer. "Sounds like another collection day for the poor, eh, Johnny boy?"

"Yes," Little John said with a smile.

Inside the carriage, Prince John let out a cackle of pleasure. His assistant, an ugly little snake named Sir Hiss, snickered, too. Why were they so happy? Because they were surrounded by bags and bags of coins! Gold and silver shone everywhere—and all of it had been taken from the poor people of England.

"Ah, taxes!" Prince John said. "Beautiful, lovely taxes!"

Sir Hiss smiled his wicked smile. He had a gap in his front teeth, just wide enough for his forked tongue to dart out when he talked. "Sire," he said, "you have an absolute skill for collecting money from the poor."

"To coin a phrase, 'Rob the poor to feed the rich!'" Prince John said with a loud chuckle. "Now tell me, what is our next stop, Hiss?"

"Nottingham, Sire," Sir Hiss answered.

"Ah, Nottingham, the richest plum of all!" said Prince John. He reached for his jeweled crown. "I shall wear this. It gives me a feeling of power."

Sir Hiss grabbed a mirror and held it up to the prince's face. "A perfect fit, Sire. How well King Richard's crown sits upon your noble brow!"

"Doesn't it?" Prince John said. But suddenly his smile

disappeared. His face became red with fury, and he clutched Sir Hiss by the throat. "King *Richard*, did you say? I told you never to mention my brother's name!"

"A . . . a mere slip of the tongue, Your Majesty," Hiss protested. "We're in this plot together, remember? And it was your idea that *I* hypnotize him—"

"And send him off to the Holy Land on that crazy Crusade," Prince John said, laughing again. He let go of Hiss, who plopped to the ground.

"Yes," Hiss said, "although it caused much sorrow for the Queen Mother."

Old Prince John behaved just like a baby at the mention of his mother's name. He stuck his thumb in his mouth and sucked it—and was that ever noisy! "Mother always did like Richard best," he whined.

"Uh, Your Highness, please don't do that," Hiss said. "If you don't mind my saying so, you have a very loud thumb."

The prince and his right-hand snake were so busy talking they didn't hear Robin Hood and Little John in the woods. Those two rascals were retrieving costumes in secret hiding places—scarves, shawls, skirts, earrings, you name it. Before long you couldn't recognize them. They looked like two exotic gypsy women! Together they popped out of the woods and started doing a wild dance.

"Oo-de-lolly, oo-de-lolly!" Robin sang.

"Fortunes told . . . good-luck charms . . . horoscopes!" Little John called out in a high-pitched voice.

Prince John peered out the curtains. "Fortune-tellers!" he said. "How droll. Stop the coach!"

But Sir Hiss was not so trusting. "Sire, they may be bandits," he whispered.

"Oh, poppycock!" Prince John retorted. "Female bandits? What rubbish!"

As the carriage stopped, he pulled open the curtains. Robin and Little John walked up to him and curtsied. "My dear ladies," Prince John said, holding out his hand, "you have my permission to kiss the royal hand."

Robin took hold of one hand; Little John, the other. And let me tell you, those hands had so many rings on them you practically couldn't see the fingers! There were diamonds, rubies, and emeralds. Not only that, but each jewel was the size of a marble.

"Oh, how gracious and generous you are," Robin said in a high-pitched voice. He kissed the prince's hand— and gently slid off one of the rings!

"Sire!" Sir Hiss whispered into the prince's ear. "Did you see what they—"

Hiss's tongue was flicking the prince's ear, and Prince John couldn't stop giggling. "Hoo hoo hee hee! Stop hissing in my ear, Hiss!"

Little John kissed the prince's other hand—and

sucked the jewels out of the rings. Then he smiled at Hiss.

Those jewels glittered like a chandelier in Little John's mouth. And that made Hiss whisper again in the prince's ear. "Your Highness—"

"Get out!" Prince John yelled. He grabbed Hiss by the neck and pulled him away. "You've hissed your last hiss!"

He quickly tied Hiss into a knot and dropped him into a basket. Then he closed the basket and sat on it. "Suspicious snake!" he mumbled.

It was time for the best part of Robin's plan. He hopped up into the carriage and pulled the curtain closed. "Masterfully done, Your Excellency," he said, seating himself across from the prince. "And now for your fortune. Close your eyes and concentrate. No peeking."

When Robin saw the bags of gold and silver on the floor, his eyes lit up. He began to chant like a fortune-teller. "From the mists of time come forth spirits . . ."

Outside the carriage, Little John had filled a glass ball with fireflies. With a string, he tied the ball to a long stick and pushed it through the curtain. "Okay, little fireflies, glow!" he whispered.

And glow they did. They made the glass ball look like a magic crystal. Robin smiled. "Look, Sire. Look!"

Prince John opened his eyes. "Incredible! Floating spirits!"

"Oo-de-lolly!" Robin chanted. "A handsome face appears, with a crown on his noble brow. It's a regal, majestic, *cuddly* face. . . ."

Robin sure knew the right words to say. Prince John was so flattered he just stared into the ball with delight. He didn't even notice Robin grabbing money bags and handing them through the curtain to Little John.

Sir Hiss saw it, though, through the wicker slats of the basket. But each time he tried to get out, the prince just pushed him back in.

Little John took the money bags and stuffed them into his costume. But as he walked away, something caught his eye. "What have we here?" he said, looking at the carriage wheels. "Solid gold hubcaps!"

Sure enough, he took off all four hubcaps and tucked them under his shirt. Then he walked up front, where the rhino guards were holding a huge treasure chest.

"Oo-de-lolly, the jackpot!" Little John said to himself.

He waved to one of the rhinos and smiled. The rhino must have thought Little John was mighty pretty, because he blushed and turned away. It was easy for Little John to sneak under the chest and carve a hole in the bottom with his dagger.

All Little John had to do was open his collar, and a pile of coins came tumbling down into his costume.

Unfortunately, one of the rhinos spotted Little John bulging with loot.

Phweeeeeeee! He blew his whistle as hard as he could.

It was time to escape! Little John ran away from the guards. At the same time, Robin rushed out of the carriage. He was carrying a money bag—and wearing the prince's robe!

Robin was looking behind him as he ran and didn't see Little John, who was looking behind *him*.

Thud! The two of them ran smack into each other. Coins spilled all over the ground. Robin scrambled to put some back in his bag, while Little John stuffed handfuls down into his costume.

Just then the carriage curtain flew open. Prince John stood there in nothing but his underwear. "I've been robbed!" he cried out.

Laughing uncontrollably, Robin and Little John turned and ran into the woods.

"After them, you fools!" Prince John shouted to the guards.

As the rhinos ran after Robin, the elephants tried to pull the carriage. But since Little John had removed the hubcaps, the wheels came right off! Prince John and Sir

Hiss went flying out the back of the carriage. With a *splat* and a *squish*, they landed in the mud.

Prince John threw a tantrum. "No, no, no, no, no!" he cried, pounding his fists in the mud.

"I knew this would happen!" Sir Hiss said angrily. "I tried to warn you, but no, you wouldn't listen."

Prince John was in no mood for a scolding. He saw that the mirror had fallen out of the carriage, so he picked it up and bonked Hiss over the head with it.

"Ouch," Hiss said. "That's seven years' bad luck. Besides, you broke your mother's mirror."

"Mommy!" Prince John cried in horror.

And the prince sat sucking his thumb, mud and all, as Robin and Little John escaped.

C H A P T E R   T W O

As you can guess, Prince John wasn't too happy about that episode. As a matter of fact, he offered a huge reward for the capture of Robin Hood.

But good old Robin just kept right on robbing the rich to feed the poor. And it was a good thing he did, because the folks of Nottingham were nearly starving to death.

Take Otto the hound, for instance. He was one of the town's blacksmiths. The poor fellow had broken his leg and missed two weeks of work. When he ran out of money, he went back to work, cast and all.

One day Friar Tuck paid old Otto a visit. Friar Tuck was one of Robin Hood's Merry Men. He was a kind old badger, roly-poly and *very* holy. He believed in doing good—even if it meant doing it behind Prince John's back!

"Good morning, Friar Tuck!" Otto called out as the friar stepped inside the blacksmith shop.

"Shh!" Friar Tuck warned, looking around carefully.

He pulled a bag of money out of his cloak. "This is for you, Otto. It's from Robin Hood."

"Oh, bless him!" Otto called out happily.

But wouldn't you know it, just then the evil Sheriff of Nottingham came walking toward the shop, humming loudly.

"It's the sheriff!" Friar Tuck cried. "Hide the money, quick!"

Otto stuffed the money right down his cast just as the sheriff barged in. "Greetings from your friendly neighborhood tax collector!" the sheriff said.

"Take it easy on me, Sheriff," Otto pleaded. "What with this busted leg and all, I'm way behind in my work!"

Friar Tuck pulled a rocking chair from the corner. "Have a heart, Sheriff," he said, sitting Otto in the chair. "Can't you see he's laid up? Come on, Otto, you'd better sit down and rest."

As Otto sat down, the coins started to jingle. The sheriff gave a crooked smile when he heard that. "I think you need to lift that leg and rest it on the table," he said. "Let me give you a hand."

The sheriff gave him a hand, all right. He lifted Otto's leg up . . . and up . . . and pulled the cast right off! Those coins came jangling out into the sheriff's greedy paws.

"Bingo!" the sheriff said with a grin. "Oh, what won't they think of next?"

Poor Otto was in pain, but the sheriff didn't care. He stuck the cast back on and said, "It smarts, doesn't it, Otto? Well, Prince John says that taxes *should* hurt."

"Now see here, you evil-hearted—" Friar Tuck began.

"Save your sermon, Preacher," the sheriff cut in. "It isn't Sunday, you know."

With that, the mean old sheriff walked right out of the shop.

His next stop was at the house of Widow Rabbit and her children. He could hear a birthday party going on, and he peeked in the window. He could see the Widow Rabbit giving a present to her seven-year-old son, Skippy. All the other children were singing "Happy Birthday to You."

The sheriff walked right in and sang along for the last part of the song. Well, those happy kids suddenly looked scared. Skippy tried to hide his present from the sheriff.

"Well, sonny, aren't you going to open it?" the sheriff asked.

Skippy took the ribbon off the box and lifted the lid. His eyes lit up. "Oh, boy!" he shouted. "One whole farthing!"

Now, a farthing isn't much money—sort of like a penny. But for those poor rabbits, it was a lot. Skippy turned the box upside down to let the coin fall into his hand.

But the sheriff just snatched it out of the air!

Little Skippy started crying, poor thing. "Have you no heart?" Widow Rabbit said to the sheriff. "We all saved to give it to him."

"Well, the family that saves together, pays together!" the sheriff said.

As he turned to go, an old blind beggar hobbled in with a tin cup. "Alms for the poor!" he called out.

You know what the sheriff did? He threw Skippy's coin into the beggar's cup, which made all the coins bounce up into the air, then he grabbed *all* the coins and put them in his own pouch. "Well, so far it's been a cheerful morning!" he said. "Keep saving!" he told the widow, and then he left.

Widow Rabbit went straight to the beggar. "You poor old man," she said. "Come inside and rest yourself."

"Thank you," the beggar said. "Tell me, did I hear someone singing a birthday song?"

"Yes, sir," Skippy said. "But that mean old sheriff took my present."

"Well," the beggar said, taking off his dark glasses and standing up straight. "I've got just the present for you!"

Skippy could hardly believe it. The beggar was Robin Hood in disguise—Skippy's hero!

Robin pulled a small bow and arrow from under his costume and held them out to Skippy.

"For me?" Skippy said. "Gee, thanks, Mister Robin Hood!" He took the bow and arrow and turned to his brothers and sisters. "How do I look, huh?"

"Not much like Mister Robin Hood," said his sister, Tagalong.

So Robin took off his hat and put it on Skippy's head. "There you go!"

"It's too big," said Skippy's other sister, Sis.

She was right, but that didn't matter to Skippy. He was thrilled. "Oo-de-lolly, I'm going to try out the bow and arrow!" he yelled, running outside.

The widow laughed. "How can I ever thank you?" she said to Robin.

"I only wish I could do more," Robin said. Then he handed her a small bag of money. "Here. And keep your chin up. Someday there'll be happiness again in Nottingham. You'll see."

As Robin left, Widow Rabbit had a tear in her eye. She hoped Robin was right.

C H A P T E R   T H R E E

kippy and Tagalong and Sis were so happy they couldn't stop running and laughing. Soon they came to the house of their friend Toby. Now, Toby was a shy little turtle who preferred reading to running. But he sure was excited when he saw Skippy's bow and arrow, and he happily joined the three rabbits as they ran along.

They stopped by a big stone wall. Everyone wanted to shoot the arrow, but Skippy insisted on going first. "Watch this!" he said, putting the arrow in the bow.

"You're pointing it too high," Sis warned.

She was right. The arrow sailed up and up . . . right over the wall! Inside that wall were the grounds of Prince John's castle and the castle tower itself. *No one* was allowed onto the castle grounds without an invitation.

"Uh-oh," Toby said. "Now you've done it! You can't go in there, or Prince John'll chop off your head."

"I don't care!" Skippy said. "I have to get my arrow!"

Skippy ran to the gate in the wall and squeezed through

it. The other kids looked on. They were so scared they could hardly breathe.

It was lucky for Skippy that he was a rabbit. He could hop along quickly and quietly on the castle grounds. Before long he saw his arrow sticking up out of the ground.

The problem was, the arrow was right near two very noisy people playing badminton. They hadn't seen the arrow, though, so Skippy sneaked up on it, closer and closer.

When he saw who the players were, he couldn't believe his eyes. One was Maid Marian, King Richard's niece and the most beautiful vixen in all the land. Everyone in Nottingham talked about how she and Robin Hood had once been in love, long ago.

The other player was Lady Kluck, Maid Marian's lady-in-waiting. She was a chicken, strong and stout, but not a very good badminton player.

"Ooops!" she said as she swung at the birdie, missing by a mile. "Where did it go?"

Just as Skippy got near his arrow—*plop!* The birdie landed inches away. "There it is!" Maid Marian called out.

The next moment, Skippy and Marian were face-to-face. "Oh! Well, hello!" Marian said. "Where did you come from?"

Skippy was shaking with fear. "Please don't tell Prince John," he pleaded.

"Don't be afraid," Marian said. "You've done nothing wrong." She stepped back and smiled. "Klucky, who does this young archer remind you of?"

"Upon my word!" Lady Kluck said, looking at Skippy's hat. "The notorious Robin Hood!"

By the gate, little Tagalong had been holding back a sneeze for the longest time. Finally she had to let it out. "Ahhhh-choooo!"

Maid Marian spun around and saw the three other children. "Don't be afraid," she said. "Please come here."

Sis whispered to the other, "That's Maid Marian. Mama says she's awful nice."

One by one, the children squeezed through the gate. Tagalong was the bravest. She went right up to Marian and said, "Mama says you and Robin Hood are sweethearts."

Maid Marian blushed. "Yes, but that was several years ago, before I left Nottingham for London."

"Did he ever kiss you?" Toby asked.

"Well, no," Marian said with a shy laugh. "And I'm afraid by now he's probably forgotten all about me."

"Oh, not Robin Hood," Skippy said. Then he reached into Toby's shell and pulled out a wooden sword.

(Meek little Toby always carried one there.) Skippy waved it in the air, pretending to be an expert swordsman. "I'll bet he'll storm the castle, fight the guards, rescue you, and drag you off to Sherwood Forest!"

Lady Kluck laughed. She picked up her badminton racket and pointed it at Skippy. "I'll be Prince John!" she said. "I hereby challenge you to a duel!"

Lady Kluck and Skippy lunged at each other in a make-believe sword fight. "Take that and that and that!" Skippy shouted.

"Oh, you got me!" Lady Kluck cried, pretending to be stabbed. As she fell to the ground, Skippy took Marian's hand and led her into the bushes. The other children followed behind.

"Oh, Robin," Maid Marian said, "you're so brave!"

Skippy looked around. "*Now* what are we going to do?"

"Usually the hero gives his fair lady a kiss," Marian said.

"A kiss?" said Skippy, wrinkling up his nose. "Oh, that's sissy stuff."

"Well, if you won't, I will," said Marian. And she picked up the squirming bunny and planted a big kiss right on his cheek.

"They're kissing!" Sis screamed.

Well, you never heard a bunch of kids laugh so hard— and you never saw a seven year old get so embarrassed!

*   *   *

Later, after the children had gone home, Maid Marian sat sadly in her room in the castle tower. All she could think about was Robin Hood.

She turned toward Lady Kluck, who was knitting quietly. "Oh, Klucky," Maid Marian said with a sigh. "Surely Robin must know how much I still love him."

"Of course, my dear," Lady Kluck answered. "Believe me, someday soon your uncle, King Richard, will have an outlaw for an in-law."

Marian looked out the window. She tried to hold back a tear. "Oh, but *when*, Klucky? I've been away so long. What if he's forgotten about me?"

They both sat there in silence for a long, long time. Little Skippy had gotten Marian to thinking. And the more she thought about Robin Hood, the more she thought her heart was going to break.

ou know what? Maid Marian had nothing to worry about. Why, at that very moment Robin Hood was in his hideout—daydreaming about her! In fact, he was daydreaming so deeply he burned the kettle of stew he was making.

Little John dipped a spoon into the stew and tasted it. "Yech!" he said. "Robin, your mind's not on the food."

"Sorry, Johnny," said Robin. "I guess I was thinking about Maid Marian again. I can't help it. I love her."

"Look," Little John said, "why don't you stop moping around and just marry her? Climb the castle walls, sweep her off her feet. Carry her off in style!"

"Ah, it's no use, Johnny," Robin replied. "It wouldn't work. Besides, what have I got to offer her? I'm an outlaw, always on the run. That's no life for a lovely lady."

Just then Friar Tuck strolled into the hideout. "You're

no outlaw," he said. "Why, someday you'll be called a great hero!"

"A hero?" Robin said, bursting into laughter. "Did you hear that, Johnny?"

"All right, laugh if you want," Friar Tuck said. "But I heard Prince John is having a championship archery tournament in Nottingham tomorrow—and Maid Marian is going to kiss the winner!"

Robin grinned from ear to ear. "A kiss to the winner!" he said. He was so happy, he started doing cartwheels. "Oo-de-lolly! Come on, Johnny, what are we waiting for?"

"Wait a minute, Rob," said Little John. "That place will be crawling with soldiers."

Robin jumped up on a table, threw his hat into the air, and then quickly took his bow and arrow in hand. With one quick, sure shot, he sent the arrow clean through the hat!

"Fear not, my friends," he announced as the hat fell back onto his head. "This will be my greatest adventure!"

hat a sight the tournament was! Hundreds of people flocked to the fairgrounds. First came a brass band of elephants. Then came the rhino guards, dressed in their finest. And behind them the entire town of Nottingham marched together. The Widow Rabbit was there with Skippy, Sis, and Tagalong, and so were Toby and his family.

There were tents galore, where you could buy pies, toys, balloons, and souvenirs. Hundreds of flags flapped in the breeze. And right in the center of it all stood a line of bull's-eye targets for the contestants.

The prince sat with Sir Hiss in a high viewing stand. They were smiling at the parade, but inside their heads was an evil plot.

"Oh, Sire," said Sir Hiss into the prince's ear. "Your plan to capture Robin Hood in public is sheer genius! Surely he won't be able to resist entering the tournament if he can win a kiss from the lovely Maid Marian."

Prince John snickered. "Yes, Hiss. My trap is baited and set. Soon I shall have my revenge!"

Too bad Maid Marian didn't hear what they were saying. She and Lady Kluck were walking toward the stand, deep in conversation. "Oh, Klucky, I'm so excited," Marian said. "Perhaps Robin is here! But if he is, surely he must be in disguise. How will I recognize him?"

"He'll let you know he's here, somehow," Lady Kluck said. "That young rogue of yours is full of surprises, my dear."

Maid Marian and Lady Kluck climbed the stairs to the viewing stand and took their seats right next to the prince. Marian excitedly looked across the fairgrounds at the contestants lining up. There was a turtle, a warthog, a pig, a dog, a duck, and a long-legged stork with a huge beak and a floppy hat. Marian's heart sank. Robin Hood was not among them.

Or so she thought.

You see, the stork wasn't a stork at all. He was Robin Hood in disguise. The stork's legs were really stilts, and the beak was a mask. Even the Sheriff of Nottingham couldn't recognize Robin.

Little John was disguised, too, in a fancy costume with a big collar. He carried a cane and wore a blond wig, a mustache, and a monocle.

Prince John wasn't the only one who had a plan. So had Robin and Little John. Step one was for Little John to become pals with the prince.

"Ah, me lord," Little John said, walking up to the prince. "My esteemed royal sovereign of the realm, the head man himself. You're *beautiful*."

Prince John sure did like to be complimented. "This fellow has style, eh, Hiss?" he said.

"And who might you be, sir?" Hiss asked Little John suspiciously.

"I am Sir Reginald, Duke of Chutney," Little John answered.

"Please, sit down," Prince John said.

So Little John sat down—right on top of Hiss. "Thanks, P. J.," said Little John. "Couldn't get a better seat than this."

Hiss squirmed out from underneath him. "You, sir, have taken my seat!" he protested.

"Hiss, get out there and keep your snake eyes open for you-know-who," Prince John commanded.

"You mean, I'm being dismissed?" Hiss asked, shocked.

"You heard His Mightiness," Little John said. "Move it, creepy. Get lost."

Sir Hiss left in a huff. But he had a job to do, and Sir Hiss always did his job. He found a bunch of balloons tied to a post and wriggled his head into one of them. He blew and blew. With all his hot air, the balloon rose into the air—carrying Hiss inside it!

The crafty Hiss used his back end like a propeller and

flew over the fairgrounds, on the lookout for Robin Hood.

Guess who spotted him? Friar Tuck and . . . *me*, Allan-a-Dale! We chased after him, but that sneaky snake kept escaping us.

Meanwhile, the archers were marching past the viewing stand. One by one, they bowed to Maid Marian. But Robin did something more. He took a daisy out of his hat and handed it to Marian. "Begging your pardon, Your Ladyship," he said in a gruff voice, "but it's a great honor to be shooting for the favor of a lovely lady like you. I hope I win the kiss!"

Old Prince John didn't recognize Robin at all. But Marian sure did. She was so in love with him she could tell it was Robin just by looking in his eyes.

She sniffed the daisy and said, "Thank you, my thin-legged archer. I wish you luck." Then she added softly, "With all my heart."

Slimy Sir Hiss was hovering above. When he saw how Marian and the stork were gazing at each other, he knew that something was up.

Just then the captain of the tournament declared, "The Tournament of the Golden Arrow will now begin!"

Rat-ta-ta-ta-ta-taahhh! Two elephants, standing on tall stone towers, trumpeted loudly.

"Hooray!" shouted the crowd.

The first group of archers stepped up. With a *whoosh*,

their arrows flew toward the targets. With a *thunk*, they landed. None of them hit dead center, but some came close.

Then came the second group, and the third. Finally the Sheriff of Nottingham himself stepped up.

A hush went through the crowd as the sheriff let loose a shot. It sailed through the air and hit the target—just a smidgen to the right of the bull's-eye.

"Boooo!" roared the crowd.

Next it was Robin's turn. He was on stilts, in his ridiculous stork outfit, and carrying a broken arrow held together with string.

Robin carefully took aim. He shot that arrow straight through the air—and smack into the center of the bull's-eye!

All the people of Nottingham roared and cheered. They didn't know the stork was Robin Hood in disguise—they were just glad to see someone beat the sheriff!

Then came the second round, and the third. Each time, Robin hit the bull's-eye.

As for the sheriff, well, he wasn't too happy. Not only was he losing, but he was losing to a raggedy-looking stork!

Robin's disguise fooled everybody—except Sir Hiss. In his balloon, Hiss managed to swoop quietly behind Robin and look under his costume.

When Hiss saw Robin's legs on the stilts, he smiled.

The minstrel, Allan-a-Dale, standing next to a poster of the most wanted fox in the land — Robin Hood, who robs from the rich and gives to the poor.

Sir Hiss flatters the vain Prince John as they ride in the royal coach through Nottingham.

Disguised as fortune-tellers, Robin Hood and Little John flag down Prince John's carriage.

Robin Hood and Little John take off with Prince John's fortune . . . and his robe, too!

No sooner does Friar Tuck slip poor Otto a bit of money than the Sheriff of Nottingham prepares to take it away.

Robin Hood daydreams about the love of his life, Maid Marian.

The sheriff and a royal rhino guard capture Robin Hood.

Little John, disguised as Sir Reginald, Duke of Chutney, forces the prince to free Robin Hood!

Imprisoned by Prince John, Robin Hood's friend Friar Tuck awaits execution.

Little John and Robin Hood (disguised as a prison guard) sneak past the snoozing sheriff to rescue Friar Tuck.

Robin Hood nabs a bag of hidden gold without waking the prince.

Sir Hiss tries to prevent Robin Hood from stealing the royal loot.

After helping to free the imprisoned citizens of Nottingham, Little John leads them to safety, with plenty of gold for all!

With King Richard back on his throne, Robin Hood and Maid Marian are free
to love one another forevermore. Oo-de-lolly!

"I can't wait to tell His Majesty!" he said to himself, floating back upward.

Just then Friar Tuck and I saw our chance. The friar found an arrow and borrowed my guitar. Using a guitar string as a bowstring, he drew the arrow back and . . .

Pop! For a holy man, that Friar sure can shoot. His arrow burst that slimy snake's balloon and sent him tumbling out of the sky—and right into the arms of Friar Tuck.

"Unhand me!" Hiss shouted. But Friar Tuck stuffed him through the small opening in an empty old keg, then closed it tight with a cork. Hiss yelled as loud as he could, but no one could hear him.

By the time we got back to the tournament, the captain was making an announcement. "Attention, everyone!" he called out. "The final contestants are the honorable Sheriff of Nottingham and the spindle-legged stork from Devonshire!"

Robin bowed toward Maid Marian as the crowd cheered. Marian waved back to him with a shy smile.

Old Prince John may have been conceited, but he wasn't stupid. The look in Marian's eyes told him that the stork had to be Robin in disguise. "My dear," he said, "I take it you favor the gangly youth?"

"Yes, Sire," Marian said, trying not to betray her true feelings. "He . . . amuses me."

"He amuses me, too," the prince said with a sinister chuckle.

"For the final showdown," said the captain, "move the target back thirty paces!"

Back thirty paces? I could barely believe my ears. That was quite a distance!

The target had a small opening in the back just big enough for a medium-sized individual to fit inside.

A vulture named Nutsy was supposed to move the target back. The sheriff pulled Nutsy aside and said, "You heard him, Nutsy. Get going—and remember what you're supposed to do!"

"Yes, sir!" Nutsy said.

Nutsy got into the target, moved it back thirty paces, and waited inside for the sheriff to shoot.

The sheriff's arrow whizzed toward the target, but about three feet too high!

Just then, Nutsy jumped. The target went up in the air, and the arrow landed in the bull's-eye.

What a cheat that sheriff was! The crowd booed their heads off, but the sheriff just grinned. "Well, that shot wins the golden arrow, the kiss, and the whole caboodle!"

Poor Maid Marian looked like her heart had been broken.

But Robin still had to take his turn. He stepped into place, lifted his bow, and took aim.

The sheriff stuck his bow between Robin's legs so that it hit the tip of Robin's bow just as he was firing.

Sprrroooing! Robin's bow tilted upward. The shot was

much too high. There was no way it could hit the target.

Robin didn't even stop to look. Quick as a wink, he pulled out another arrow and shot it.

The second arrow sliced through the air so fast you could hear it whistle. It was way too high, too!

But it was *supposed* to be too high. It caught up to the first arrow, grazed it, and tipped it downward.

Now the first arrow was heading right toward the target. Everyone in the crowd held their breath.

Thwock! Not only did the arrow land in the bull's-eye, but it split the sheriff's arrow clean in half!

"He did it! He did it!" Friar Tuck shouted.

Let me tell you, that crowd went crazy! The cheering was as loud as thunder.

The rhino guards escorted Robin to the viewing stand. Marian looked like she wanted to run up to Robin and kiss him right then. But first the prince had to make an announcement.

Robin bowed low. The prince reached out with his sword as if he were going to dub Robin a knight. The crowd hushed.

"Archer," Prince John said, "because of your superior skill, I hereby name you the winner."

The rhinos came closer. An ugly grin spread across Prince John's face. "Or more appropriately," the prince continued, "the loser."

With a quick thrust, the prince stuck his sword under

Robin's shirt and ripped it off. Robin's costume fell to the ground, and there he was, standing on those tall stilts for all to see.

"Seize him!" the prince bellowed.

Robin tried to get away, but the rhino guards grabbed him. They wrestled him to the ground and tied him up.

"Have mercy," Maid Marian pleaded. "I beg you to spare his life. I . . . I love him, Your Highness."

Prince John chuckled. "Oh? And does this prisoner return your love?"

"Marian, my darling," Robin said in a loud, clear voice, "I love you more than life itself."

"Ah, young love," Prince John said with a sigh. "Fear not. Your pleas have not fallen upon a heart of stone."

Maid Marian's eyes lit up. Was the prince going to forgive Robin?

"But traitors to the Crown," the prince went on, "must die!"

"Traitor to the Crown?" Robin said. "That crown belongs to King Richard. Long live King Richard!"

"Long live King Richard!" thundered the crowd.

That really made Prince John furious. "Enough!" he screamed. "I am king!" Then he whirled around to the rhino guards, his face red with anger. He pointed to Robin and roared, "Off with his head!"

t looked like it was all over for Robin. The rhinos led him off to the chopping block. An executioner was waiting there with a huge ax glinting in the sun.

Maid Marian's beautiful face was white as ash. She collapsed into Lady Kluck's arms, weeping.

All the townspeople stared in horror. It was so quiet you could hear your heart beat. Robin knelt down, and the executioner raised his ax.

Then Prince John blurted out another command. "Executioner, stop! Hold your ax!"

Well, you would have thought the whole town had frozen. No one moved an inch. I thought I was hearing things.

But I wasn't. You see, behind Prince John was a big curtain—and behind the curtain was Little John. He held Prince John by the collar with one hand and pointed a sharp dagger at him with the other. "Okay, big shot," he whispered to the prince. "Now tell him to untie my buddy, or I'll—"

"Ah, Sheriff," Prince John said, scared out of his wits, "release my buddy—ah, I mean, release the prisoner!"

The sheriff couldn't believe his ears. "Untie the prisoner?"

"You heard him, Bushel Britches!" Lady Kluck yelled.

The rhinos untied Robin, and he ran toward Maid Marian. The two of them hugged so tight I wondered how they could breathe. All around them, the crowd hooted and cheered.

But old Bushel Britches suspected something was wrong. During all the noise, he sneaked behind the curtain and saw Little John.

"Why, you—" he snarled, drawing his sword.

Little John saw him coming. He let go of Prince John and ducked just in time, then took off as fast as his big old body could carry him.

"Kill Robin Hood!" shrieked the prince.

The whole place went wild. People began running in all directions while Robin fought off the guards with his sword. Prince John, that old coward, hid behind the keg that held Sir Hiss.

Lady Kluck grabbed Maid Marian's hand and ran for cover. When the sheriff tried to stop her, she flipped him right over her shoulder.

Suddenly Robin swooped down on a vine and swept Marian up in his arms. Up they went, to the safety of the canopy above the viewing stand. "Marian, my love," Robin said, "will you marry me?"

"Oh, darling, I thought you'd never ask!" Marian replied.

With a smile on his face, Robin leapt back out on the vine and plunged back into the fight.

A few yards away, Little John pushed a bunch of rhino guards into a tent. A moment later, Lady Kluck stuck a spear into the tent—and did those rhinos start to run! The trouble was, they were still inside the tent, so they couldn't see where they were going! They crashed into Little John, they crashed into the sheriff, and they knocked down the stone towers. Meanwhile, Lady Kluck was mowing down rhino guards with her powerful body. The whole place was falling apart—and the townspeople loved it. They were screaming with happiness.

In all the confusion, Robin, Maid Marian, Little John, Friar Tuck, Lady Kluck, and I managed to sneak away into the woods.

No one saw us escape. Not even Prince John, who was still hiding behind the keg. He looked around and grumbled, "Hiss, you're never around when I need you."

Hiss's voice answered from within the keg. "Coming!"

Prince John turned in surprise. He pulled the cork and out popped Hiss. Hiss said, "You won't believe this, Sire, but the stork is really Robin Hood!"

Prince John stared at him. "Robin Hood," he said through clenched teeth. "Some help you are!"

In a burst of anger, the prince tied Hiss into a knot around a nearby pole. "Get out of that, if you can!"

As the prince walked away, Hiss dangled there, wondering what he had done wrong.

And that's what happened at the archery tournament. It was a big day for Robin Hood. He won the contest, he won Maid Marian, and he made a fool of the sheriff and the prince.

Little did he know what was to come.

 id we have a party that afternoon! There was dancing, singing, and lots of good eating. Music was provided by me, of course, with the help of a few other musicians.

Friar Tuck and Little John had sneaked back into town and invited Otto the blacksmith, the Widow Rabbit and her family, Toby and his family, and all of our other friends.

It was a happy time for everyone. But the happiest of all were Robin and Marian, dancing away and looking like two lovebirds. It did my heart good to see them.

I wished those high spirits could have lasted forever. But I'm sad to say, things were about to get worse.

Much worse.

At that very moment, the prince was having a tantrum in his castle. The sheriff and Sir Hiss were there, and even they had to shrink away in fear.

Crash! Prince John threw a vase into a mirror. "They all laughed at me!" he screamed. "Now they mock me in the streets! Well, they'll be singing a different tune!" He grabbed Sir Hiss tightly and said, "Double the taxes! Triple the taxes! Squeeze every last drop out of those insolent peasants!"

Prince John sure did make good on those threats. His subjects paid dearly for making him look like a fool. Why, he taxed the very heart and soul out of the people of Nottingham.

And if you couldn't afford the taxes . . . you went to jail. The Nottingham jail became so crowded you could hardly move. I should know, because I ended up there. So did Widow Rabbit and her family, Toby and his family, Otto—in fact, just about everybody who was at the tournament.

A few people did manage to stay out of jail. One of them was good old Friar Tuck. Every Sunday, Friar Tuck would ring the church bell, and the sexton, a mouse who lived in the church wall, would play the organ. And every Sunday, fewer and fewer people would show up.

Finally, one rainy Sunday, the sexton said, "Friar, I don't think anyone is coming."

But Friar Tuck kept on ringing the bell. "You're right, Sexton," he said. "But maybe the sound of the bell will bring those poor people some comfort. We must do what we can to keep their hopes alive."

No sooner had he spoken than the sexton's wife scurried

out of a hole in the wall. She was holding a farthing. "Friar Tuck, we've saved this," she said. "It's not much, but please take it for the poor."

"Your last farthing?" Friar Tuck said. "Little sister, no one can give more than that." He took the coin and dropped it into the church's poor box, which had been empty. "Bless you both."

Well, who should walk in at that very moment but old Bushel Britches himself! Why, that sheriff could practically *smell* money.

"Howdy, Friar," the sheriff said. "It looks like I dropped by just in time." He opened up the poor box and took out the farthing. "Well, what have we got here?"

"Now just a minute, Sheriff!" Friar Tuck said. "That's the poor box!"

The sheriff laughed. "It sure is," he said. "And I'll just take this for poor Prince John."

"You thieving scoundrel!" Friar Tuck said. "Collecting taxes for that arrogant, greedy, ruthless, no-good Prince John!"

"Take it easy, Friar," the sheriff answered. "I'm just doing my duty."

"Get out of my church!" Friar Tuck shouted. Oh, he was hopping mad. He picked up his cane and began hitting the sheriff. "You want taxes? I'll give you taxes!"

The sexton was shocked at the friar's behavior—but

impressed, too. "Give it to him!" he yelled with glee.

And that's how Friar Tuck landed in jail. The sheriff called it high treason to the Crown.

Just about everyone who lived in Nottingham was in jail now. Everyone, that is, except one very important person.

Robin Hood.

No matter how hard Prince John's men tried, they couldn't find Robin in Sherwood Forest. The prince's mood got worse and worse. He would stay in his counting-house for days, glumly pacing back and forth.

Sir Hiss tried to make the prince feel better. The day Friar Tuck was arrested, Hiss walked into the counting-house with a smile. "Sire, the taxes are pouring in from the rest of the kingdom, and the jail is full," Hiss said. "Oh, and I have good news. Friar Tuck is in jail."

"But it's Robin Hood I want!" Prince John bellowed angrily. Then suddenly he got quiet. "Friar Tuck . . . hmmm, I can use that fat friar as bait to trap Robin Hood. Yes, that's it! Friar Tuck will be led to the gallows in the village square."

"B-b-but, Sire," Hiss said, "you really mean to hang Friar Tuck, a man of the church?"

"Yes, you silly serpent!" Prince John said. "And when Robin Hood tries to rescue him, my men will be ready!"

CHAPTER EIGHT

t was an evil plan, all right. Even Sir Hiss was shaken by it. But the prince knew the perfect cold-hearted person to put in charge—the sheriff.

The sheriff used Nutsy and another vulture named Trigger to help him build the gallows, right outside the castle gate, in full view from the prison windows.

Just as they were hammering in the last nail, an old beggar walked up to them. He was wearing dark glasses and feeling his way around with a cane.

Yes, it was Robin Hood, but the sheriff and his helpers didn't know that.

"Alms for the poor!" Robin said in a crackly voice. "Do me old ears hear the voice of the sheriff?"

"That's right, old man," the sheriff said.

"What be going on here?" Robin asked.

"We're going to hang Friar Tuck at dawn," the sheriff answered.

Nutsy laughed. "Yep, and maybe it'll be a double hanging!"

Robin was stunned. He knew Prince John was a scoundrel, but he didn't think he was low enough to hang a friar. "A double hanging, huh?" Robin said, remembering to speak in a hoarse voice. "Who be the other one who gets the rope?"

Trigger jumped off the gallows. He pulled out his bow and arrow and aimed at Robin. "Sheriff, he's getting too all-fired nosy!"

"Aw, I didn't mean anything," Robin said. "But, uh, couldn't there be trouble if Robin Hood showed up?"

"Well, what do you know?" said Nutsy with a chuckle. "He guessed it!"

"Nutsy, button your beak!" Trigger ordered.

But Robin knew just the right thing to say. "Oh, no need to worry. The sheriff is too clever for the likes of Robin Hood."

Old Bushel Britches swelled up with pride. "You hear that, Nutsy?" he said.

"Sheriff, I still have the feeling that snoopy old codger knows too much," Trigger said.

"Get back to work, Trigger," the sheriff replied. "He's just a harmless old blind beggar."

That "harmless old blind beggar" kept walking along the castle wall. Just out of sight of the gallows, Little John was waiting for him.

"Rob," Little John whispered, "we can't let them hang Friar Tuck."

Robin took off his glasses. "A jailbreak tonight is the only chance he's got."

"A jailbreak?" Little John said. "There's no way you can get over the castle wall and into the jail!"

"We've got to, Johnny," Robin said. "Or Friar Tuck dies at dawn."

They waited until darkness, hiding in the shadow of the castle wall. Along the top of the wall, guards patrolled back and forth. Robin and Little John waited until the guards were out of sight. Then they made their move.

They dragged over a ladder that they had found in Otto's shop. Then they set it against the wall and climbed up. Crouching low, they could see Trigger, Nutsy, and the sheriff guarding the jail. Actually, just Trigger and Nutsy were guarding it—the sheriff was fast asleep against the jail door.

As they jumped to the ground, Little John knocked loose some stones from the wall. He and Robin ran into the shadows, hoping nobody had heard them.

But that old buzzard Trigger had sharp hearing. "Sheriff," he called out, "I've got a feeling in my bones there's going to be a jailbreak any minute."

Trigger was standing with his crossbow pointing directly at the sheriff. When old Bushel Britches opened his eyes, he said, "Trigger, will you point that peashooter the other way?"

"Don't you worry, Sheriff," Trigger said confidently. "I put the safety on."

With a smile he tapped the crossbow. *Booiinnggg!* An arrow flew out and barely missed the sheriff's head. It ricocheted from the castle wall to the jail wall and back.

Meanwhile, Nutsy was off patrolling. As he approached Robin and Little John's hiding place, Little John grabbed him. He put his hand over the vulture's mouth, and Nutsy let out a muffled "Oof."

Back at the jail door, Trigger said, "Did you hear that?"

"I sure did, Trigger," the sheriff replied. "There's something funny going on around here. Come on."

Trigger and the sheriff walked carefully along the wall until they saw a dark shape in the shadows. "You in there," the sheriff ordered, "come out with your hands up."

Robin Hood did come out—but with Nutsy's uniform on and with a sock over his nose that looked just like a vulture's beak!

"Trigger, put that peashooter down!" said Robin, in a perfect imitation of Nutsy's voice.

"Aw, shucks, Trigger," the sheriff said, "it's only Nutsy. Now get back to your patrol."

Trigger slinked away, muttering to himself.

"I'm telling you, Nutsy," the sheriff said to Robin, "that Trigger's getting everyone all edgy."

Robin spotted a chair by the castle wall. He pulled

it over and said in Nutsy's voice, "Sheriff, why don't you just sit yourself down here and get cozy?"

"Why, thank you, Nutsy," the sheriff said, settling into the chair.

"Just close your sleepy eyes," Robin said. Then he started singing, "Rock-a-bye, Sheriff . . . just you relax . . ."

In a minute or two, the sheriff fell asleep. Robin carefully snatched the keys from his belt and sneaked toward the jail door.

Suddenly old Bushel Britches snorted and sat up. Robin froze in his tracks.

"Aw, Nutsy, that's mighty sweet," the sheriff said, with his eyes still closed. "Sing it one more time, will you?"

Robin tiptoed back. As he hummed the lullaby, he waved toward Little John.

Little John got the message. He came over and took the keys. Then he unlocked the door, stepped inside, and closed it.

Or, I should say, *slammed* it. That door let out a noise that sounded like a gunshot.

Up on the wall, Trigger started screeching, "Jailbreak!" He fired another of his wild shots, and the arrow went ricocheting off everything in sight.

As the arrow whizzed by the sheriff, he jumped up from his chair. "What's going on?" he demanded.

"I heard it, Sheriff," Trigger said. "The door!"

The sheriff spun around, but all he saw was a closed door with Nutsy (or, I should say, Robin) standing guard. He folded his arms and walked toward Trigger. "For the last time, Trigger, no more false alarms!"

Robin turned toward the door. "Psst, Little John!" he whispered.

Little John stuck his head out the door. "Yeah, Rob?"

"You release Friar Tuck and the others," Robin said, "and I'll drop in on the Royal Treasury."

"Right!" Little John turned around and bounded up a stone staircase. At the top, he saw a door marked Death for Treason.

He peeked inside and saw Friar Tuck chained to the wall.

"Friar!" Little John shouted. He ran in and began unlocking the Friar's shackles.

"Oh, Little John!" Friar Tuck exclaimed. "My prayers have been answered!"

"Shh," Little John said. "We're busting out of here."

I'm happy to say that the next prisoner he unlocked was none other than yours truly. Soon Little John and Friar Tuck had unchained Otto, Widow Rabbit and her family, and everyone else in that whole dreary prison.

Now here comes the amazing part. Robin Hood, with a long rope wrapped around his shoulders, was climbing all the way up the castle tower. At the very top was

Prince John's bedroom. Inside, the prince was sleeping soundly, with all his bags of gold stacked neatly on the floor. Sir Hiss was also asleep, in a basket at the foot of the bed.

Robin Hood had an idea—an idea that would put the prince's money back in the hands of the townspeople.

Robin carefully climbed in the bedroom window and quietly tied his rope around one of his arrows. He drew the arrow back and prepared to shoot it toward the jail.

Suddenly the prince's voice rang out, cutting through the still night. "ROBIN HOOD!"

 obin was determined to follow his plan. He quickly let his arrow fly. It flew down, down, down—and straight into the window of our jail cell, with the rope trailing behind it.

Then he whirled around, prepared for the worst.

But the prince was still in bed, tossing from right to left. "I'll get even with him," he mumbled. "I'll get . . . rrrrahhgghg . . ."

He was talking in his sleep! Robin breathed a sigh of relief.

Meanwhile, Robin's arrow had wedged itself between some stones in our cell wall. Little John pulled it out, wrapped the rope once around a heavy table leg, then put the arrow in his bow and shot it back toward Robin.

It sailed back through the prince's window and stuck in the ceiling. Robin pulled it out, untied the rope from the arrow, looped it around a hook in the wall, and tied both ends together.

I told you that Robin was the smartest fox around. Now he had a long pulley system running from the tower window to the jail window, something like a clothesline. One by one, he tied the money bags to the rope—and sent them on down to the jail!

When we prisoners saw that money coming in, we cheered.

"Praise the Lord and pass the tax rebate!" Friar Tuck called out.

We had never seen so much money in our lives. We stood there running our fingers through the coins. Finally we'd be able to buy food and clothing again, thanks to Robin! I caught a glimpse of Widow Rabbit hugging her children and sobbing with joy.

But Little John knew the sheriff wouldn't stay asleep forever. "Come on," he said. "Follow me."

A group of prisoners took their bags and followed him downstairs toward the door. There was no time to lose.

One of the bags on the line had a hole in it, and coins began to spill out—right down on the sleeping sheriff!

Sure enough, he sat up and opened his eyes. "What the—" he began.

But Little John was quick. He opened the door, put his hand over the sheriff's mouth, and pulled him into the jail.

Of course, Trigger had heard the commotion. He came running toward the jail door.

He thought the sheriff was waiting there, but he was

wrong. Little John had tied the sheriff up and taken his uniform—and now he looked just like old Bushel Britches! As Trigger came close, Little John pretended to be waking up.

"Sheriff, now don't get angry," Trigger said, "but I've still got a feeling the—"

Little John reached out his paw and grabbed Trigger. "Friar!" he called over his shoulder. "Get going! Hurry!"

The friar and the first group of prisoners raced out of the jail, clutching the money bags.

As for Robin, well, he was loading the last money bag onto the line when he spotted another bag under Prince John's pillow. At first he thought he'd leave it. But you know Robin, always ready for a challenge. He crept up to the prince's bed, lifted the pillow, and swiped the bag.

"Oh!" the prince cried out. But he fell right back to sleep, happily sucking his thumb.

As I said before, when the prince sucked his thumb, you could hear it a mile away. Unfortunately for Robin, Sir Hiss was asleep only a few feet away, at the foot of the prince's bed. The noise woke him right up.

"Stop, thief!" Hiss shrieked.

Holding the money bag, Robin grabbed on to the line. But before he could get through the window, Hiss leapt up, dug his teeth into Robin's bag, and pulled!

Back in the jail cell, we kept pulling the rope. But after Hiss grabbed Robin, we couldn't get the line to move. "Pull harder!" I yelled.

Up in the tower room, Hiss had wrapped his tail around the nearest object—Prince John's foot. "Oh!" Prince John cried out, waking up. "Oh! Oh! Oh!"

We all gave a good hard yank. Robin came out the window pulling Hiss, who was pulling the prince.

As Prince John was being pulled out of bed, he managed to grab hold of one of the bedposts. But he and the bed were dragged onto the terrace, and the prince was pulled over the edge and left hanging on to the railing by his fingertips.

"Guards! My gold!" howled Prince John.

What a sight! As Robin hung from the line, just next to him was Hiss, holding on to a bag of gold with his teeth. His back end was still wrapped around Prince John's leg. Meanwhile, from the top of the castle wall, the prince's guards were firing arrows all around Robin.

Robin quickly began to pull himself hand over hand along the rope toward us.

We gave one more hard yank, and in flew Robin through the jail window, followed swiftly by the remaining bags of gold. But Prince John came in a little too low. He smacked right into the jail wall and fell to the ground, outside the jail door.

Happy prisoners ran past him, carrying their money bags. "Oh, no, no, no!" the prince shouted. "They're getting away with my gold! Guards! Guards! Charge the jail!"

Prince John scrambled to his feet and slammed the jail door shut. When he turned around, he saw the rhino guards doing just what he'd told them to do—charging the jail. But they didn't see that the prince was directly in their path!

The prince turned white with terror as the guards' spears came nearer. "Rhinos!" he called out. "Halt! Stop! Desist!"

Wham! The rhinos' spears dug into the door—above, around, and under the prince. The door came clean off its hinges, with the prince trapped between the spears. As the rhinos kept on charging, the prince yelled, "Yiiiiii!"

At the same time, Robin was scampering down the jail stairs. "Everybody, this way!" he called.

The prisoners sped out of the jail as fast as their legs

could carry them. The guards kept shooting, and arrows kept falling down like rain.

Robin and Skippy crouched by the door and fired back. *Whoosh! Whoosh! Whoosh!* Each of Robin's shots hit its mark. His arrows pinned the guards against the castle wall by their shirts.

Friar Tuck and Little John were doing their jobs, too. The friar was wheeling prisoners away in a big cart. Little John managed to topple over a stack of barrels, which rolled toward the rhino guards.

Crash! The kegs knocked those rhinos over like bowling pins!

Robin ran to the castle wall. There was only one sure way to get everyone to the other side—by lowering the drawbridge. Quickly, Robin found the handle that controlled the drawbridge. He flicked it, and the drawbridge dropped downward.

We were free! Some of the prisoners ran over the bridge and out of the castle grounds. Friar Tuck, Little John, and Robin pushed the rest over in the cart.

"On to Sherwood Forest!" Friar Tuck shouted.

Just then we heard a small voice behind us. "Mama, Mama, wait for me!"

"Stop!" Widow Rabbit shouted. "My baby!"

It was Tagalong! The poor thing was still on the castle grounds. She was running toward the drawbridge, holding on to her little doll for dear life!

Robin ran back over the bridge so fast his feet barely touched the ground. He scooped Tagalong up into his arms, then turned to escape. Rhinos were gaining on him, and arrows kept pouring down. He ran toward the drawbridge, gritting his teeth and covering Tagalong as best he could.

Suddenly I looked up and noticed the iron gate that hung between Robin and the bridge. It seemed to be shaking.

I looked down and realized why. The crocodile who was captain of the archery tournament was cutting the rope that held up the gate.

Little John saw it, too. "No!" he shouted.

But it was too late. With a loud *clang*, the gate crashed down. Robin and Tagalong were trapped!

CHAPTER ELEVEN

e got him now!" the sheriff called out.

Little John left the prisoners and ran up to the gate. Since Tagalong was so small, Robin was able to squeeze her through the iron bars and push her into Little John's arms.

"Got you!" Little John said. "But Rob—"

"Don't worry about me!" Robin insisted. "Keep going!"

Little John turned and ran. Robin spun around to face the rhino guards. They were a few feet away from him, their heavy axes raised high over their heads.

Clannnnkkk! When those axes hit the gate, the sound was like an explosion.

They missed Robin by a long shot. He was already near the top of the gate, climbing as quick as a lizard.

But he wouldn't be safe for long. He was surrounded. His eyes darted right and left until he saw the rope that he had used to pass all the prince's money to the poor. He grabbed it and swung over the heads of the guards.

Whump! Robin slammed into the sheriff, knocking him

off his feet and against the rhinos. They all fell to the ground in a heap.

"Oo-de-lolly!" Robin shouted as he sailed to the top of the wall. But the guards were after him again. The prince was after him. Even the sheriff had gotten to his feet and was chasing him.

No matter where Robin went, arrows whizzed by him. He ducked and jumped, barely getting out of the way. He leapt from wall to wall. He swung from ropes. I must admit, I didn't think he would make it.

Finally Robin was cornered in front of the tower. He leapt onto a window ledge and began to climb up the tower wall.

Down below, the sheriff grinned a slimy, nasty grin. "This time we got him for sure!" he said, and ran inside the tower.

The tower stairway was lit by small torches on the wall. The sheriff grabbed one and ran up the stairs.

Robin scaled the tower until he reached Prince John's treasury room. Then he climbed inside, safe and sound.

But not for long. Seconds later, the sheriff barged in through the door and said, "I think this room needs more light." He touched the torch to the room's curtains.

With a loud *whoosh*, the curtains went up in flames!

Summoning all his courage, Robin leapt through the fire and out the window. Grabbing on to the ledge again, he moved higher and higher up the tower.

Prince John and Sir Hiss had climbed to a lower balcony on the tower. When they spotted Robin, the prince screamed, "Shoot him!"

Back on the ground, I held my breath. Friar Tuck's face was pale with fear. Skippy looked like he was about to cry.

Robin was on the tower roof, surrounded by flames. Below him, the guards were shooting like crazy. If an arrow didn't get him, the fire surely would. There was no place to go!

Except down.

And down Robin went, leaping over the side of the tower. I covered my eyes. I couldn't bear to see my good buddy—*splaaaaassh!*

I opened my eyes. There was a huge, round ripple in the castle moat—right where Robin must have jumped in.

"Kill him!" Prince John's voice was hysterical. "*Kill him!*"

Dozens of arrows splashed into the water, making bull's-eyes in the center of the ripple.

Little John and Skippy ran to the edge of the water. "Come on, Rob," Little John said, trying to see any sign of Robin. "Come on."

"He's got to make it!" Skippy said.

Finally something came to the surface. It was Robin's hat.

There was an arrow right through it.

CHAPTER TWELVE

o," Little John said in a hoarse whisper. "Oh, no!"

Prince John and Sir Hiss were standing at the gate now, their eyes glued to the water. "Hiss, he's finished!" the prince cackled. "He's **done** for! Hoooo-ha-ha-ha-ha-ha!"

Skippy's mouth was hanging open in shock. He grabbed Little John's paw and started to cry.

And you know what? That tough old bear had tears in his eyes, too. Robin was the best friend he ever had.

Little John was about to turn away when he saw something strange in the water—a little hollow piece of wood, sticking straight up and moving slowly toward him.

Little John squatted down and leaned over the water. "What's that?"

Squirt! A spurt of water shot from the stick, right into Little John's face!

"Hey, what the—" Little John sputtered.

And who should pop out of the water but Robin Hood! Without his hat—but *alive!*

Skippy let out a squeal of happiness that nearly broke my eardrums. He jumped straight into Robin's wet arms.

The rest of us did a little whooping and hollering, too, I must say.

"Oh, did you have me worried, Rob," Little John said. "I thought you were long gone."

"Aw, not Robin Hood!" Skippy said with a big grin. "He could have swum twice that far!"

But not everybody was happy. By the castle gate, Sir Hiss was staring in disbelief. "Look, Sire," he said. "He's made it. He got away again."

How did Prince John react? You guessed it. He threw a tantrum. "No, no, no!" he cried, falling to his knees and pounding his fists on the ground. "It's so miserably unfair!"

Hiss shook his head in frustration. "I tried to tell you, but no, no, you wouldn't listen. Your traps never work. And now look what you've done to your mother's castle!"

Prince John turned to look. The tower was ablaze. It looked like one huge roaring flame.

"Mommy!" Prince John screamed, sticking his thumb in his mouth. "Oh, it's all your fault, Hiss!"

"My fault?" Hiss said. "*I* was right all along."

The prince stood up and reached for Hiss's neck. "I'll get you!"

"No, Sire, please!" Hiss said, running away. "Help! Help me, someone! He's gone stark-raving mad!"

And that was the last we saw of those two that day—running around the castle grounds, screaming at the top of their lungs.

It was a funny sight. And it was a great day for Nottingham.

Well, the story has a happy ending, folks. King Richard finally returned to England and straightened everything out. He promptly put Prince John and Sir Hiss in jail, and to this day they're probably still pounding rocks in the royal rock pile. And they're probably still arguing over something or another.

As for Robin, he married Maid Marian in Friar Tuck's church. It was the prettiest ceremony I ever saw. Skippy was the ring bearer and Tagalong was the flower girl.

Little John and Lady Kluck were so happy at the wedding, I thought they'd cry, but the proudest person of all was Marian's uncle, King Richard. As the happy couple left for their honeymoon, I saw him put his arm around Friar Tuck and say, "Ah, Friar, it appears that I now have an outlaw for an in-law, eh?"

The king had a hearty laugh, and we all laughed along with him. The sound echoed through Sherwood Forest, and let me tell you, a sweeter sound was never heard!